For Connor Mancini

Scholastic Children's Books
An imprint of Scholastic Ltd
Euston House, 24 Eversholt Street
London, NW1 1DB, UK
Registered office: Westfield Road, Southam, Warwickshire, CV47 0RA
SCHOLASTIC and associated logos are trademarks and/or registered trademarks of Scholastic Inc.

First published in the US by Scholastic Inc, 2010
This edition published in the UK by Scholastic Ltd, 2010

HB ISBN 978 1407 12388 2
C&F ISBN 978 1407 12400 1

A CIP catalogue record for this book is available from the British Library.

Printed in the UK by CPI Bookmarque, Croydon, Surrey.
Papers used by Scholastic Children's Books are made from wood grown in
sustainable forests.

3 5 7 9 10 8 6 4

www.scholastic.co.uk/zone

A SCIENTIFIC DISCLAIMER

By

Professor Gaylord M. Sneedly

The book you hold in your hands contains many scientific errors and stuff.

For example, dinosaurs and cavemen did not live at the same time. Dinosaurs lived more than 64 million years BEFORE cavemen.

And I should know! In 2003, I was the recipient of The Most Brilliantest Science Guy of the Whole Wide World Award.

So there!

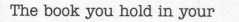

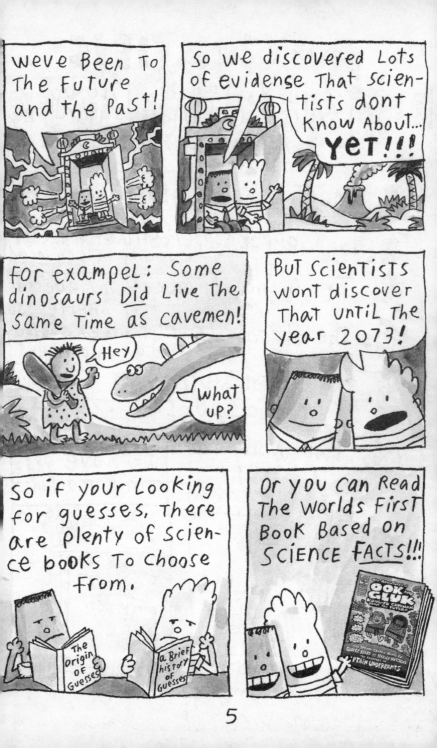

CHAPTERS

The Adventures of OOK and GLUK
KUNG-FU CAVEMEN FROM THE FUTURE

CHAPTER 1
Meet OOK and GLUK

This is Ook Schadowski and Gluk Jones. Ook is the kid on the left with the missing tooth and the stringy haircut. Gluk is the kid on the right with the lepard spots and the afro.

remember that now!

Ook and Gluk lived way back in the year 500,001 B.C. in a village called Caveland, Ohio.

welkum to Caveland

8

Another time when they were 7, they almost got ate up by Mog-Mog: The fearsest dinosaur in Caveland.

SUCKAAA!
And once they even traveled to the future, learned kung-fu, and saved there whole villege from evil robots and time-traveling weirdos!
But before we can tell you that story, we have to tell you
This story

This is BiG cheif Goppernopper.

He was the Ruler of caveland and He hated Ook and GLuk.

Grrrr

Every time chief Goppernopper Tried to be a big shot, Ook and GLuk always ruined it!

clank clank

Look at me! Me invented wheel!

SHOOM

Look at me! me created spear!

SNAP

BOOM

Look at me! me Discovered FIRE!

ZOOoooOM

14

17

22

23

24

25

26

27

Hey ya Pee-Brain Goof Juice!
YA Twinkel Toes!
ya Porky-Pine!
Hey, ya Ginger snap!
ya Big oL dumb Monkey!
ya bluebery!
Danger Quick Sand
DANGER QUICK SAND
DANGER QUICK SAND
SPLA
DANGER QUICK SAND

29

30

32

FLIP-O-RAMA

Here's How it Works!!!

STEP 1
Plase your Left hand inside the dotted Lines marked "Left Hand HERE." Hold the Book open FLAT.

Step 2
GRasP the Right-hand Page with YOUR Right Thumb and index finGeR (inside the dotted Lines marked "RigHt ThumB Here").

STEP 3
Now Quickly FLip the Right-hand Page back and FOURTH Until the Pitcher apears to Be Animated!

(For extra Fun, try adding your own sound afecks.)

35

FLIP-O-RAMA #1
(Pages **37** and **39**)

Remember, flip <u>only</u> page **37**. While you are fliping, be shure you can see the pitcher on page **37** <u>And</u> the one on page **39**.

IF you Flip Quickly, the two pitchers will start to look like <u>one</u> animated pitcher.

Dont Forget to add your own Sound Afecks.

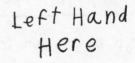

Left Hand Here

Do the Bite Thing

37

right thumb Here

Do the Bite thing

40

CHAPTER 2

OOK

The Goppernoppers STRIKE BACK

GLUK

42

43

44

...you will end up in the year 2222 AD. This is where Im from. Welcome to the Headquarters of Goppernopper Enterprises.

Here, have a complamentery coffey mug and mousepad.

awesome.

But me no understand how come you need Time Portal?

48

49

51

FLIP-O
RAMA 2

Left hand
Here

Bunches-o-Punches!

RIGHT THUMB Here

Bunches-o-Punches!

56

58

60

STOP THEM!

meanwile...

EXIT

soon our heros found themselfes running for their lifes in a strange futuristic city from the future.

Here they come!

stop or me shoot!

me too!

Quick hide behind this sign.

our

62

64

65

That night, Master Wong's daughter, Lan, cooked a big dinner. Ook and Gluk told them everything that happend.

What we do now?

Hmmm...

You must stay ~~hear~~ her and Learn the Ways of Kung-Fu.

Then when you are ready, Perhapse you can help your family and freinds.

68

69

70

The next Day
Hey whats your pet dinosaurs name anyway?
Ummm...
She no really have name, me guess.
Well Im going To call her LiLy cuz Lilies are my faverite flowers.
OK
Today we begin your inst-ruckshon. What is it you wish to Learn?

Me want to Learn how to Kick butt.
me too.
Those who Kick butt are weak. For violens has no mind.
aw man!
If you truley want to set things right, you must walk the Path of Peace.
Here are two white Belts. they are simbels of your dedicashen To your Training
cool.

75

Ook and Gluk studied math, sciense, grammer, speling and chemistry.

$$22\overline{)462} \quad 21$$
$$44$$
$$154$$
$$\times\ 23 \quad 22$$
$$462 \quad 22$$
$$3080$$
$$3542$$

$$\Delta t' = \gamma \Delta t = \frac{\Delta t}{\sqrt{1 - v^2/c}}$$
$$\gamma = \frac{1}{\sqrt{1 - }}$$

They also studied important Things, too.

music and art are like eating and breathing.

One cannot trulely live without them.

Even when Ook and Gluk wern't studying, they were still Learning.

Your minds are free to follow theyr'e own paths. They may soar to the heavens or rot in a prisen. Its up to you!

He who conquers his own mind is the Greatest warrier.

The mind is stronger than the flesh. It can defeat any oponent, no matter how strong.

Gopper-Nopper Tower

kung-fu fever

RIGHT
Thumb
Here

Kung-Fu Fever

Even Lily Tried to Learn the ways of Kung Fu --- but every time she spinned around, she threw up.

FLIP-O-RAMA 4

Left hand Here

Lily Loses Lunch!

87

RIGHT
thumB
here

Lily Loses Lunch!

91

Years came and went, and Ook and Gluk grew bigger and stronger all the time.

even Ooks missing tooth grew back in.

me Look wesome!

in your dreams!

93

94

CHAPTER 4

The Heros Jerney

Seven years had come and gone. In that time, Ook and Gluk had grown into men.

the time now come for us to fase us's destir

O.K.

Lets go.

oh Ook, Be carefull!!! Dont get hurt!!! I couldent Bear it if anything bad happened to you!

Hey what about us?

oh yeah. you too.

96

97

99

Ook, Gluk, and Lily walked threw the poluted city toward Goppernopper Enter-prises

these new Black Belts really cool... but me still a little woried.

Remember what Master Wong sa: "Dont...umm...Dont scared and stuff."

But they got Lazer guns and Torcher machines

Master Wong say: "Brains is more awesome than other umm... stuff. Brains can d feet ever strongest enemy guy.

Master Wong talk better than you.

Yeah me know Him have wa with words

Ook's Rebuke!

RiGhT
ThumB
Here

Ook's Rebuke!

GLUK AMUCK!

107

GLUK Amuck!

113

Regergitation
Animation

Right thumb here.

Regergitation
Animation

124

127

129

130

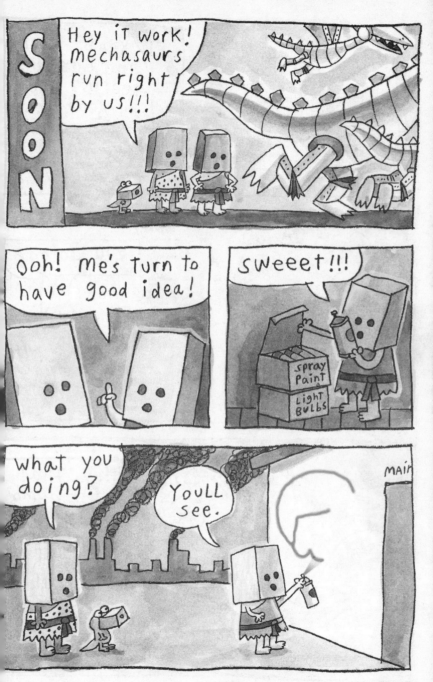

133

135

Mechasaurus
Wrecks!

Right
Thumb
Here

Mechasaurus
Wrecks!

POW
Gopper-Nopper Tower
PUNCH
RIP
CRIK
KRUM-BLE
Gopper-Nopper Tower
CRACK
FOOSH
HooRay!!! Goppernopper Tower destr-oyed Forever!
Hey
wher
LiLy
at?

142

With Goppernopper Enterprises in Flames and the mechasaurs destroyed, Ook and Gluk vowed to Re-Bild their world.

ZAP

499,944 B.C.

They started by sending chief Goppernopper and his evil Workers back to the year 2229 AD.

aw, man!

ZAP

B.C.

now it time to find your mom!!!

143

147

152

153

The Pain Event!

RIGHT
THUMB
Here

The Pain Event!

master Wong turned and walked back home.

it was a Jerney he had walked many Times.

...but This Time was more like a dream

165

So OOK, GLUK, Lan and Lily started off on thier Long WALK to CaveLand.

and before too Long, they ran into a old friend.

Learn to Speak
caveman Language!!!

CAVEMONICS

It Fun! | It easy! | it Annoy Grown-ups!

Lesson #1 | Turn "I" into "Me"

Want to talk Like Caveman? First Rule: No more use Pronoun "I". Instead use "Me".

Lets Practise!

ENGLISH		CAVEMONICS
I Like candy.	=	Me Like candy.
I play baseball.	=	Me play baseball.
I am awesome.	=	Me awesome.

Lesson #2 | Simplify

Drop any unnesessary informashon. Also, try to find simple replacements for words with more than two sylables.

Lets Practise

ENGLISH		CAVEMONICS
I dont care for anchovies on my pizza.	=	Me no like little fishes.
I'm going to the local Amusement park today.	=	Me go to Barf ride place.
I'd like to eat at Applebees.	=	me go to Barf place.

LeSSoN #3 — Avoid contractions

Stay away from words like "don't," "can't" and "haven't."

Instead try to use the simplest form of the word as a replacement.

In many cases, "no" will do just fine.

chalk

Lets Practise

ENGLiSH	CAVEMONICS
I can't spel very well.	= me no spel good.
I haven't done my homework.	= Me do homework. Dog eat it.
My Grandmother doesn't think this book belongs in the school Library.	= Grandma no fun.

The Ook and Gluk Adventure Continues Online AT WWW.PILKEY.COM AND WWW.SCHOLASTIC.COM

Watch a film about how the book was made!

COOL!

Learn how to draw Ook, Gluk, Lily, the Mechasaurs, and MORE!

Free Downloads!
Free Video Games!

Free!

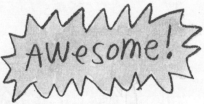

AWesome!

Meet the "REAL" Lily!

195

About The Author and Illustrator

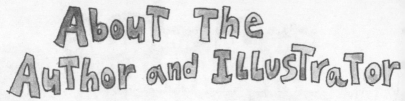

GEORGE BEARD (age 9³/₄) is the co-creator of Captain Underpants, Super Diaper Baby, Hairy Potty, and The Amazing Cow Lady.

In his spare time, George enjoys skateboarding, playing with his two cats, and making comic books with his best friend, Harold Hutchins.

For the past seven months, George has taken Kung-Fu lessons at Master Wong's School of Kung-Fu in Piqua, Ohio. George currently wears a green belt.

HAROLD HUTCHINS (age 10) is a fourth grader at Jerome Horwitz Elementary School. He has written and illustrated more than 30 comic books with his best friend, George Beard.

In his spare time, Harold enjoys skateboarding, drawing, watching movies, and chewing gum.

Harold takes classes at Master Wong's School of Kung-Fu. Recently, Harold earned the title of purple belt although he is keenly aware that it's "not about the belt."